PRIMEVAL

THE
LOST
PREDATOR

PRIMEVAL
THE LOST PREDATOR

Adapted by Alicia Brodersen

PUFFIN

PUFFIN BOOKS

Published by the Penguin Group

Penguin Books Ltd, 80 Strand, London WC2R ORL, England

Penguin Group (USA) Inc., 375 Hudson Street, New York, New York 10014, USA

Penguin Group (Canada), 90 Eglinton Avenue East, Suite 700, Toronto, Ontario, Canada M4P 2Y3
(a division of Pearson Penguin Canada Inc.)

Penguin Ireland, 25 St Stephen's Green, Dublin 2, Ireland (a division of Penguin Books Ltd)

Penguin Group (Australia), 250 Camberwell Road, Camberwell, Victoria 3124, Australia
(a division of Pearson Australia Group Pty Ltd)

Penguin Books India Pvt Ltd, 11 Community Centre, Panchsheel Park, New Delhi – 110 017, India

Penguin Group (NZ), 67 Apollo Drive, Rosedale, North Shore 0632, New Zealand
(a division of Pearson New Zealand Ltd)

Penguin Books (South Africa) (Pty) Ltd, 24 Sturdee Avenue, Rosebank,
Johannesburg 2196, South Africa

Penguin Books Ltd, Registered Offices: 80 Strand, London WC2R ORL, England

puffinbooks.com

First published 2008

2

Text copyright © Impossible Pictures, 2008
Photographs copyright © Impossible Pictures, 2008
Adapted by Alicia Brodersen
All rights reserved

The moral right of the author has been asserted

Set in Times New Roman
Typeset by Palimpsest Book Production Limited, Grangemouth, Stirlingshire
Made and printed in England by Clays Ltd, St Ives plc

British Library Cataloguing in Publication Data
A CIP catalogue record for this book is available from the British Library

ISBN: 978-0-141-32393-0

THE
LOST
PREDATOR

CHAPTER 1

Today was turning out to be a very good day for Andy. Not only was he already several holes ahead of his game partner, Jeff, but now – as he veered round a corner in his golf buggy – he could see the fairway stretching ahead, down towards the stately Victorian manor that doubled as the club house. If he played this next shot right, he'd be straight on to the green and back inside the club for lunch.

'Tiger Woods.' He smiled smugly to himself. 'Eat your heart out!'

Andy jumped out of the buggy and placed a tee in the grass. Pulling out his favourite club, he put the ball into place and lined up the shot. Unfortunately, it took three missed shots before Andy finally got it right.

Thwack!

A grin spread across Andy's face as the ball and club connected, sending the small white sphere

3

spinning into the air. But as he watched in dismay, the ball arched and headed downwards, straight into a water hazard a few metres away from the right of the green.

Andy shook his head in disbelief. What a way to ruin a perfect day. His mobile began to ring in his pocket. It was Jeff, wondering if Andy was on the green yet.

Andy looked back at the pond his ball had just fallen into.

'Yeah,' he bluffed, squinting in the sunshine. 'Easy.'

Andy closed his phone and headed purposefully towards the water. If he didn't find the ball soon, Jeff would beat him to the eighteenth and he wouldn't hear the end of it for months.

Andy inched towards the edge of the water trap, carefully putting his hand into the murky green water as a slight breeze whistled through the bullrushes at the edge of the pond. Feeling around in the mud, Andy soon found the ball and pulled it out.

It was just as well Andy wasn't really paying attention to his surroundings. Because down there in the pond, twisted among the water weed and smiling a grey, lifeless grin, lay the bones of a baby deer.

From the puncture wounds in its skull it was clear the unlucky creature hadn't died of natural causes. And now it was lost forever, buried in a watery grave.

CHAPTER 2

Connor Temple smiled satisfactorily at the breakfast laid out on the tray before him. A ripe plum, a freshly brewed pot of coffee, a fluffy croissant . . . yes – *this was the life*! Standing in the kitchen in his dressing gown, Connor couldn't have been happier.

He'd been staying at his friend Abby Maitland's place in London for a month now, and he loved it. He was sleeping on the sofa – after he'd been kicked out of student digs for not being able to keep up with the rent.

But Abby loved animals and had a job as a keeper at Wellington Zoo, which meant that her home decorating reflected her lifestyle. It really was something else.

Connor loved the cactus plants lined up beside the radiators. He loved the lizard posters and kooky creature ornaments that hung along the walls. He even loved all the reptile pets that lived in glass boxes at various points around the main living room.

But most of all, Connor loved the fact he got to see Abby every day. He'd had a massive crush on her since the moment they'd met. Connor was convinced that the longer he stuck around, the sooner Abby was going to realize how much she liked him too!

Connor took the breakfast tray in both hands, just as Abby came walking through the door, rubbing her eyes. As always, she was wearing the skimpy clothes she'd been sleeping in.

'Morning!' she smiled sleepily, eyeing the breakfast tray. 'Aw . . . you shouldn't have!'

'Shouldn't have what?' Connor said, oblivious to her hint. He inched around her. 'Excuse me!'

Abby put her hands on her hips as she watched him leave the kitchen. The cheek of him! Abby thought back to when Connor had turned up uninvited on her doorstep, begging for a place to stay for a few days. And now he'd been here a month and couldn't even be bothered to make her *breakfast*!

Abby followed Connor into the living room, intending to ask him how much longer he'd be staying. But something was wrong – the room felt so hot! Abby looked at the thermostat on the wall.

'Thirty-four degrees?' she cried.

Connor averted his eyes and scuttled nervously

over to sit at the dinner table in the middle of the room.

'Yep,' he replied breezily, as he began to wolf down his breakfast. 'Rex was looking a wee bit chilly.'

Connor began to feel a little sheepish as Abby glared at him. Even though they both knew the temperature of the flat needed to be warm for Abby's reptile collection, she obviously didn't believe him.

'The way I see it,' he added cheekily, 'if we get too hot, we can just take a bit more kit off, can't we?'

Abby sighed as she looked over at her pet dinosaur Rex. He was thirstily slurping at a water bowl on top of the glass box that doubled as his home. The small reptile looked *too* hot, if anything – the thin, lime-coloured crest on his head opening and closing like a Chinese fan, his long green body swaying from side to side as his transparent wings stuck firmly by his sides. The flying Coelurosauravus returned Abby's gaze and happily licked its lips. Connor noticed Abby's expression softening and decided to try again.

'If that little fellow gets too cold, well . . .' he said, casually pouring himself a coffee. 'I couldn't bear it if anything happened to him, Abby . . .'

Connor snuck a glance at his friend and was relieved to see she was having second thoughts. He was the only other person that knew Abby had kept the little dinosaur that she'd found in the Forest of Dean when she'd been called out to investigate a strange lizard sighting. There was no way she'd sacrifice Rex's welfare for anything.

'Yeah, right,' she said, heading off to the kitchen to fix herself some breakfast.

Connor smiled. Did he have Abby sussed or what? If she could see how much he cared about Rex, then surely she was going to see how much he cared about her too. It wouldn't be too long now before she realized he was *perfect* boyfriend material!

Back at the golf course, Andy and Jeff had finally met up. Andy was driving his buggy along the fairway and feeling superior – in more ways than one.

'Jeff,' Andy was saying in a condescending tone. 'You could have got your own buggy. You didn't have to be such a tightwad, did you?'

'Oh, come *on*,' said Jeff, pulling his golf bag wearily behind him in the hot sun. 'Give us a lift.'

Andy gave his golfing partner a pitying look. 'Come on, then,' he said, with a glint in his eye. 'Hurry up.'

But just as Jeff went to pull his golf bag up on to the cart, Andy put his foot to the accelerator and took off. Laughing, he watched as the figure of a clearly irate Jeff grew smaller in his rear-view mirror.

A few minutes later Andy wasn't in such a good mood. Once again, he was having trouble with his golf swing. This time, the ball had veered off into a patch of trees, way off the side of the green.

Andy walked into the undergrowth and started searching through shrubs. *Ouch!* He pulled his hand back in shock when a thorn ripped into his finger. Andy shook his hand in pain as drops of blood flew from the wound and landed on a nearby tree. How annoying! Now he had no ball *and* a bad golf hand. How was he going to beat Jeff back to the club house now?

Andy trudged out of the trees and back on to the green. He looked across the course for his friend, but there was no one in sight. Andy started walking towards his tee, only to be distracted by a noise that seemed to be coming up fast behind him. Andy turned round but there was no one on the ground. Instead, he was horrified to see a large shadow descending rapidly from the sky towards him. What on earth was *that*?

Whatever it was, it was coming straight for him. A petrified Andy dropped his club and started pelting down the fairway.

Seconds later, as he lined up a shot further up the green through the trees, Jeff stopped mid-swing as a blood-curdling scream split the air. He ran through the shrubs and back on to the fairway, only to be confronted by the most horrific thing he'd ever seen. There, lying on the edge of the undergrowth, was a body. It was clear from the bloody wounds that the person was dead.

Jeff inched closer. A wave of nausea came over him as he noticed the body's golf shoes. They looked horribly familiar.

They were Andy's.

CHAPTER 3

'I'm off to yoga!' Abby said, emerging from her bedroom dressed in sweats.

'Right,' said Connor absentmindedly. 'Well – any time you need help with your bending or with your stretching, give me a call.'

Abby stood in front of the television, forcing a smile. She was used to Connor dropping stupid hints about how much he liked her, and she'd long ago learnt to ignore them.

'Windows shut at *all* times,' she reminded him, looking over at Rex as he flexed his wings.

Connor mumbled in agreement and leant over, trying to look around her as his game progressed on the telly without him.

'Get in and leave by the same exit,' Abby continued firmly, picking up her yoga mat. Connor responded by waving her out of the way.

Abby glared at him, annoyed. Honestly – he was

impossible. It was like talking to a child. She'd have to get him to move out in the next couple of days, or else he was going to drive her *crazy*! Abby stormed out of the flat, slamming the front door behind her.

Connor paused the game to watch her go as Rex fluttered over to the couch and perched beside him. The young man looked at the tiny dinosaur and grinned.

'She likes me, Rex,' he smiled, misinterpreting Abby's irritation completely. 'Oh yeah . . . she likes me bad!'

'*Four hours?*' Claudia Brown was pacing through the gardens of the manor that housed the golf club, berating Captain Ryan of the SAS as the rest of his soldiers surged throughout the surrounding woodland.

'I told you to seal the perimeter – not drystone wall it!' Claudia huffed, annoyed at how long things were taking. If her boss at the Home Office, James Lester, got wind of this, she'd be in big trouble. 'I want it done in an hour. Where's the golfer's body?'

'In the casualty clearance centre in the main house,' the captain replied, unfazed. He knew she'd been thrown in at the deep end when all this dinosaur business surfaced. Considering she was one of the younger staff members of the Home Office he admired the tough way she'd handled it so far. Besides, he was used to her brisk method of dealing with things.

It had been over an hour since Jeff had made his gruesome discovery. Given the severity of the attack, the local police had quickly realized it was a much more serious case than they could handle. The SAS had immediately been called in to investigate. Now, Ryan, the captain of the squad, and Claudia were surveying the scene.

Instructing Ryan to keep her briefed on any updates, Claudia made her way over to an ambulance parked at the front of the manor. The victim's friend, wrapped in a red blanket, was clearly in shock. Professor Nick Cutter, a palaeontologist from the Central Metropolitan University, was listening intently to Jeff's version of events. Cutter ran the Department of Evolutionary Zoology at the college, and had helped discover the very first anomaly that had opened in the Forest of Dean several months ago.

As he saw Claudia approaching, Cutter left Jeff in the hands of one of the paramedics.

'What did he see?' she demanded, her pretty face looking authoritative.

'It was all over by the time he got there,' replied Cutter, slightly bemused by Claudia's lack of greeting. Like Ryan, he was used to her getting straight to the point. But there were other qualities about Claudia Brown that Cutter was beginning to warm to.

'Any sign of the anomaly?' Claudia pressed.

'We don't know for sure there *is* one yet,' said Cutter firmly, watching Claudia raise a sceptical eyebrow. 'I need to see the victim.'

Claudia stared at the older man's rugged features. They had been working together for some months now, and she was starting to like him. But they were so *different*. Here she was, a professional young woman with her hair nicely done, wearing a smart white jacket and slacks with a rose-coloured blouse. Cutter, meanwhile, gave the impression that he had never set foot inside an office – he was unkempt and unshaven in a faded grey T-shirt and jeans. Although, Claudia had to admit to herself, he *was* rather attractive. And he was the person Britain was relying on to help them through this terrible threat.

Claudia smiled to herself as she remembered that a couple of months ago, she hadn't even known what an anomaly was. But now she'd got used to the strange calls telling her yet another dinosaur had travelled through the 'doorways in time', as Nick called them. Prehistoric creatures had been arriving in present-day Britain through these large rips in the atmosphere for a while now. It certainly wasn't your average day at the office.

'Look, I think I should warn you . . . Lester's getting impatient,' Claudia said carefully, reminding Cutter of the prime minister's man in charge of the investigation. 'He thinks you cause as many problems as you solve.'

'And what do *you* think?' replied Cutter with a slight smile.

'I think it could be helpful if we could show him we're making some sort of progress,' Claudia challenged.

'Or what?'

'Or . . . it becomes difficult.' Claudia frowned as concern crept into her dark brown eyes. 'Please don't make me take sides, Nick.'

Cutter watched as Claudia turned and strode purposefully back over to the SAS unit, further down the manor's gravel driveway. He was beginning to like her too, but she could be so stubborn – much like her boss.

James Lester was a government man who didn't

know why the anomalies were happening, but just wanted Cutter to make them stop. Cutter didn't trust him, mostly because Lester and his people thought they were in control of the situation. They didn't like to think that one scientist could know more than they did. And sometimes, Cutter could see Claudia behaving the same way.

Cutter checked his watch as he walked back over to the ambulance. It was time to call in the rest of his team.

Back in Abby's flat, Connor was still playing his computer game when the phone rang.

'Abby Maitland's Love Shack!' greeted Connor, picking up the receiver. 'Number One Stud speaking!'

Connor's face fell as he heard the voice at the other end of the line. It was the professor, asking him to get down to the golf club right away.

Connor threw down the phone and ran to get dressed, cursing his stupidity. He was the one who had originally persuaded the professor and his lab assistant, Stephen Hart, to investigate the dinosaur sighting that had led to them finding the first anomaly.

That's where the three of them had met Abby too

– it was while she was investigating a strange lizard sighting that she'd stumbled upon Cutter, Stephen and Connor. So by default the four of them had become a team, cobbled together to explore the dinosaur phenomenon. But Connor had always felt Cutter saw him only as a student and not as a peer. And he knew saying stupid things on the phone wasn't going to help his cause.

Within a minute Connor was heading out of the flat. He was so excited about the new anomaly that he didn't even stop to say goodbye to Rex. Instead, he just grabbed Abby's car keys and slammed the front door behind him.

A curious Rex watched Connor leave. It didn't take long for the little creature to notice the open window above the radiator, swaying back and forth in the breeze.

Outside in the street, Connor got into Abby's Mini and leant over to the passenger side to grab hold of the *A-Z* from the dashboard. Pinpointing the fastest route to the golf course, he quickly straightened up and pulled the door shut. Connor started the car and sped off down the road.

Connor was completely oblivious to the fact that a little, green Coelurosauravus had silently flown from the window of the flat above, through the open door of the car and was now perched quite happily on the back seat.

CHAPTER 4

Claudia quickly turned away, unable to comprehend what she'd just seen. Behind her, an SAS agent pulled the white sheet back over the remains of Andy, laid out on a medical stretcher in one of the rooms of the manor.

'Any idea what might have done this?' Claudia asked Cutter.

'A creature of devastating power and savagery,' Cutter remarked, shaking his head. 'To do that in just a few minutes . . .'

Claudia and Cutter looked at each other. They knew exactly what this meant. Whatever the creature was, it must have come through an anomaly. And it was still out there.

In a hillside clearing by the rough a few moments later, Cutter and Stephen were joined by Abby, who'd been mid-yoga stretch when she got an urgent call to come out to the golf course. She'd managed to throw on a pair of trousers and a loose singlet on her way, but she looked underdressed compared with Stephen and Cutter, in their sensible outdoor canvas jackets and jeans.

'No trampled or broken vegetation, no track marks and no sign of any anomaly,' Stephen was saying as they walked through thick grass beside the rough. 'But there is an incredibly strong magnetic field, so it's got to be here somewhere.' He handed the compass in his hand over to Cutter.

But Cutter was sure something wasn't quite *right*. He spun round to face his young team as realization dawned on him.

'Quiet!' he said, almost shouting.

'We didn't say anything!' Abby protested, shooting Stephen a confused look. She practically melted when Stephen smiled back at her. His movie-star looks and muscular build made Abby seriously weak at the knees.

'No! I mean –' said Cutter excitedly, lowering his voice to a whisper. 'It's *too* quiet. Listen – there's no bird song!'

The three of them stopped talking. Cutter was right – all that could be heard was the sound of leaves rustling in a slight breeze.

'What would scare the birds away?' Cutter said, as he turned the compass round in his hands. Suddenly, he looked at Stephen. 'You were wrong. There *is* an anomaly.'

'Where?' the young lab assistant shrugged.

A smile spread across Cutter's face as he looked upwards to see a familiar shimmer spreading across the sky.

'We're standing right underneath it.'

They craned their necks in fascination. Set against the sunlit, blue sky, peppered with clouds, this one looked even more impressive than any of the anomalies they had seen before. Abby couldn't stop herself from letting out an appreciative gasp as the splintered shards of light danced above them in a circular formation.

'It's an aerial predator,' explained Stephen, realizing now what they were up against.

'That's one way of putting it,' muttered the palaeontologist, turning his attention to another area of the skyline as he walked towards the rough. 'Now, how on earth do we cordon off the sky?'

'Er, Cutter,' stuttered Stephen, as he watched an ominous silhouette pass through a patch of clouds overhead.

But Cutter was wrapped up in his own thoughts. 'I mean, this *thing* could be anywhere by now!' he continued obliviously, walking away from the group.

Their eyes fixed on the sky, Abby and Stephen started to back towards the professor as the enormous figure of a flying reptile became clearer, swiftly diving down through the air towards them.

'I wouldn't be so sure about that!' Stephen shouted, turning just in time to crash-tackle the professor to the ground before a screeching shadow swooped over them. The three lay on the ground for a second, watching in awe as the reptile glided away down towards the green.

Cutter scrambled to his feet, breaking into a grin. What a magnificent creature! The flying reptile's wing-span was at least nine metres wide, its back covered in dark fur with two salmon-coloured stripes running the length of its body. A large, red crest protruded from its head, finished off by a long, slim beak. He'd never seen anything like it.

'So!' Stephen quipped as he stood up and dusted himself off. 'Not so hard to find, then!'

Connor could see SAS soldiers guarding the entrance as he drove down the country lane towards the golf course. He smiled. Connor loved being on the team and this was his favourite part.

'Access all areas, I think you'll find,' he grinned, flashing his card at the soldier as he drove up to the barricade. The soldier eyed the boy in the Mini sceptically. With his battered trilby, fingerless gloves, maroon vest and duffle coat littered with buttons and sewn-on scout patches, he certainly didn't *look* like a government agent. Still, the soldier figured, what did he know? Maybe dinosaur hunters looked more like scruffy students these days.

'Thank you very much!' whistled Connor as the SAS soldier reluctantly waved him through.

The soldier watched as the Mini disappeared in the direction of the golf club and shook his head in disbelief. Was that *really* a flying lizard staring at him from the back window? It couldn't be. With all this talk of crazy creatures he must just be imagining things.

Connor drove into a deserted car park and got out of the Mini. Pulling off his coat, he turned round to throw it back through the driver's seat window and was stunned to come face to face with an effervescent Rex, bouncing around happily on the roof.

'Oh *my* –' he cried, startled. Rex took a step back and flattened his brilliant green crest against his head in fright. 'Sorry . . . I didn't mean to shout,' Connor tried to speak calmly. The last thing he wanted was to scare Rex off. 'I was just a bit shocked – that you're here.'

Rex chirped and looked questioningly at Connor, who was starting to panic. What was Abby going to say? She'd throw him out of the flat if she knew he'd let Rex go!

'I mean, it's *lovely* that you're here and everything,' continued Connor, his voice wavering nervously. 'But it's probably best that you stay in the car, mate. Yeah?'

Connor continued talking, trying to sound calm as he realized how absurd it must look – he was trying to reason with a flying reptile!

Rex straightened up on his front legs and waved his long green tail from side to side. Connor looked at him anxiously. He didn't have all day to play games. It was now or never.

Connor lunged, trying to grab hold of the reptile's long body. But Rex was too quick. He flexed his wings and launched himself off the roof of the Mini, gliding over the car park and through a gap in the hedge beside a fairway.

Connor had no choice. Groaning, he chased after him.

CHAPTER 5

Back by the rough, Cutter, Abby and Stephen watched as the massive creature continued to fly around the course below them. They had identified it as a reptile from the Pterosaur family. This particular one was known as a Pteranodon, which meant the anomaly must be open to the mid-Cretaceous period.

'Is it what killed the golfer?' Abby asked, as Cutter watched the elegant creature through his binoculars.

'I'd say it's definitely in the frame,' Stephen answered.

However, Cutter wasn't so sure. 'The Pteranodon was supposed to have mainly eaten small reptiles and fish,' he insisted.

'Probably just snacking until humans came along,' Stephen scoffed.

They watched as the creature suddenly seemed to

change its course. It began to circle, looking for a suitable roost.

Elsewhere on the golf course, Connor was having troubles of his own. Rex was playfully darting out of reach every time the hapless Connor tried to grab at him as they ran through the shrub.

'Rex!' Connor said breathlessly, as the two of them finally came through the trees and on to the green. 'I swear, when I catch you, you're going to become the first animal to become extinct twice!'

Rex cheeped cheerfully and flitted over to the sand trap in the middle of the fairway.

Further up the course, Stephen gasped as he noticed a familiar figure floundering through the bunkers.

'Is that *Connor*?' he said, taking a step forward.

'What's he *doing*?' cried Abby, failing to notice her pet also skipping around on the fairway.

'More importantly,' said Cutter worryingly, raising his binoculars to look at the Pteranodon in the sky. 'What's our friend up *there* doing?'

'It's not looking for a roost,' said Stephen, his eyes widening as the creature began circling just above Connor. 'It's looking for lunch!'

28

The three of them began shouting, urging their friend to get under cover.

Down on the green, Connor's heart sank as he heard yelling coming from further up the course. Looking up from the bunker, he could see the small figures of Abby, Cutter and Stephen waving at him.

'*Connor!* Come here *quickly*!' Cutter hollered desperately. When it became obvious Connor couldn't hear him, Cutter called out to Captain Ryan and Claudia, who had been searching the grounds nearby.

Connor winced. *Now* he was in trouble. Even though he couldn't hear what they were saying, they'd obviously seen him with Rex, which meant he was going to get a real talking to. After nearly being thrown off the team a few weeks ago when his friends Tom and Duncan followed him to an anomaly, Connor realized he was looking down the barrel for a second time . . . and all because of a pig-headed lizard!

'Great,' he said, waving his hands at Rex. 'That means "Game Over"!'

But Rex wasn't going anywhere. Instead, he was lowering his body to lie flat on the golf course, looking at something over Connor's shoulder. His normally gleeful chirrup became urgent. Connor turned round and suddenly lost all thought of catching the lizard.

29

Because there, screeching as it came towards him and Rex from the sky at breathtaking speed, was something that obviously wanted to catch both of them!

Stephen's voice instantly registered, loud and clear.

'*Run, you idiot!*'

Abby, Stephen and Cutter watched helplessly as Connor belted across the green, the hungry Pteranodon metres away from him. Claudia quickly took control of the situation, commanding Captain Ryan to raise his weapon.

'Shoot it!' she ordered, as another band of SAS personnel readied their guns beside her.

'No, *wait*!' Cutter raised his hand. 'There's something that doesn't add up. I'm just not entirely sure what it *is* yet.'

Claudia glared at him. Was he completely insane?

'Do it!' she urged the captain.

'*No!*' Cutter insisted. 'We should only kill these creatures when there's absolutely no other choice!'

'*What* other choice?' Claudia reckoned, pointing at the figure of Connor as he zigzagged across the grass. 'In a matter of seconds, Connor's going to be ripped to shreds!'

Claudia turned to Captain Ryan and demanded he follow orders. But as Ryan took aim at the winged reptile, Cutter threw himself against the captain, sending his fire off target. Ryan steadied himself and tried another shot, but the creature was already out of range and too focused on its own target to notice.

Unfortunately for Connor, the flying dinosaur could move faster than he could run. With one final burst of its mighty wings, the creature opened its long, powerful beak and leant down to claim its prey.

It was in that instant that Connor and Rex found themselves falling through the air, not realizing they'd been hurtling towards the edge of the seventeenth hole as they tried to escape their pursuer. As the Pterosaur had leant down to scoop them up, both Connor and Rex had tumbled over the edge. The frustrated creature missed them by mere centimetres as they landed on the grass and watched it fly off above them.

Cutter, meanwhile, was observing his young charge through the binoculars. He wasn't happy with what he saw.

'Wait a minute,' Cutter said, as he got a better look at who – and what – exactly was on the green. 'There's a *lizard* with him!'

'Ooh,' Abby groaned, momentarily forgetting no

one knew she'd rescued the small reptile when it had returned from the anomaly in the Forest of Dean. 'He let Rex escape!'

Abby's mouth dropped open as she realized she'd just blown her own secret.

'What have you *done*?' Claudia cried furiously. If everyone just kept dinosaurs they'd found wandering around, it could seriously jeopardize the whole operation. 'What do you think we're doing here? Running a private zoo?'

'You *kept* him?' added Cutter incredulously. He was also disappointed – surely Abby knew better than that. Cutter had always been adamant that all creatures who came through the anomalies should be returned. Who knew how even one tiny dinosaur from the past could affect the future?

Abby tried to think of an excuse but it was no use – she couldn't lie to Cutter. 'He came back,' she stuttered. 'I was just looking after him!'

Claudia threw her arms up in the air in frustration. She'd had it with these dinosaur-crazy people.

'Lester was right!' she ranted, shaking her head. 'You people are a menace! What do you think we're doing here, Nick – playing some kind of *game*?'

'I'm sorry, guys,' Abby whispered, looking like she

was about to cry. Now she was going to lose Rex forever.

'Nobody is taking this more seriously than we are,' Cutter yelled back at Claudia, suddenly losing his cool. Why did she always have to be so melodramatic?

Claudia ushered the SAS unit back to the golf club, as Stephen looked at the professor curiously.

'She's got a point,' he said finally.

'I'm not being sentimental,' Cutter shot back, keeping his eye on the horizon as the Pteranodon dipped out of view. 'There were good reasons for not killing the creature.'

'And you're sure of that?' wondered his lab technician out loud.

'Well, of *course* I'm not sure!' Cutter exploded. Stephen was his most trusted ally. It wasn't like him to second-guess Cutter, and it made the professor angry.

Lowering his voice, Cutter looked away. 'I've probably made the biggest mistake of my life. It's just a hunch . . . that's all.'

Connor had now reached the top of the hill, whooping with delight. He was too wrapped up in his own jubilation to notice the icy atmosphere around him.

'Wooh!' he shouted, jovially patting Cutter on the back with a bit too much familiarity. 'That was a bit of a laugh, wasn't it?'

Cutter fixed him with an unimpressed glare and shook his head. Connor obviously had no idea how much trouble he'd just caused them.

The professor stormed off to follow Claudia and the SAS unit back to the manor.

'What?' Connor asked stupidly, turning to Abby for an explanation. But Abby was too upset about Rex and didn't want to talk to him either. She needed to explain herself to Cutter.

'Hey, look . . .' Abby said, as she caught up with the professor on the edge of the rough. 'I just didn't want Rex to be locked up. To be poked and prodded by Lester's people.'

Abby looked up at Cutter shyly. His scowl seemed to be softening and it looked like he understood. Abby bit her bottom lip before adding, 'Can I keep him?'

Cutter scanned the golf course behind them.

'You better *find* him first,' he pointed out, before walking off after Claudia.

Abby watched him go as a wave of fear rose in her chest. Cutter was right – the Pteranodon was still out there. But where on earth was Rex?

CHAPTER 6

Cutter paced back and forth across the gravel driveway of the manor, talking out loud as SAS agents patrolled the area around him. Stephen and Captain Ryan were working on computers set up on the bonnets of their vehicles.

'The Pteranodon hunted from high vantage points,' Cutter explained. 'Cliff tops, mountains, anywhere that gave it a good sight of potential prey.'

'We need to be looking at all the highest points within a couple of miles,' Stephen directed, nodding to Ryan as the captain listened intently to his radio headset.

'Real-time images coming through now,' Ryan said urgently, as a series of satellite pictures began downloading on to Stephen's laptop screen.

Scrolling through the shots, Stephen finally zoomed in on the familiar outline of the Pteranodon. It looked like it was resting on the rooftop of an office block in the south of the city.

'Less than a mile away,' said Ryan, as the satellite controllers confirmed the location Stephen had pinpointed. 'Should be empty on a Saturday,' the captain called to his team standing at various points around the golf club driveway. 'Let's go!'

But Cutter still had a feeling something wasn't quite *right* – that this wasn't the creature they were after. He couldn't let Ryan and his men kill it.

'We've got to get there first!' he muttered to Stephen frantically, while Claudia hopped in the back seat.

As Abby and Connor began searching for Rex back at the golf course, the Department of Evolutionary Zoology cruiser screeched into a dark side street in Battersea. As Cutter and Claudia jumped out, Stephen quickly offloaded a serious-looking firearm. Claudia was torn between going with them or waiting for Ryan, but the other two were already at the entrance. She knew they wanted to get to the Pteranodon before Ryan and his squad.

Frustrated, Claudia followed them into the high-rise building. She needed to keep an eye on them.

As they travelled up in the lift to the top floor of the building, Claudia noticed Stephen's over-sized weapon.

'It's a tranquillizer gun,' he admitted.

Claudia came to an immediate halt. She'd calmed down after the episode on the golf course earlier, but this was too much. For goodness' sake – there was a killer on the loose!

'No way!' she shouted. 'I'm not taking any more chances – I want it dead!'

'Just trust me. Please,' Cutter said earnestly. 'Killing these creatures without good reason is *not* the answer.'

Claudia looked from Cutter to his loyal sidekick Stephen, who was standing defiantly behind his boss with the tranquillizer gun in his arms. She took a deep breath. There was no way she was going to win this argument.

'You've got until Ryan gets here,' she said ruefully. 'One chance – one shot.'

Claudia rolled her eyes as the two men grinned triumphantly and gleefully raced off down the corridor.

Up on the rooftop a few minutes later, the adult Pteranodon flexed its wings, its brilliant red crest glowing brightly in the sunlight as it surveyed the city. But just as Stephen took aim with the tranquillizer, the flying reptile spied him. With one mighty screech

37

it launched itself from the side of the building and glided off into the maze of office rooftops below them.

'We're going to have to find a way of bringing her back into range,' Cutter said, watching as the magnificent creature circled above them. It really was an awesome sight.

He breathed in deeply. What was the best way to attract a prehistoric reptile? Cutter's eyes fell upon the Pterosaur's lustrous crest, glinting in the sunshine. Cutter turned round, looking intently at his team.

'I need your shirt,' he said suddenly, motioning to Claudia's rose-coloured top.

Claudia's jaw dropped. 'What?' she said, mortified.

But Cutter wasn't going to take no for an answer. He'd already begun searching around the rooftop for something to use as a makeshift pole.

Stephen watched out of the corner of his eye as a red-faced Claudia reluctantly took off her jacket. He might not trust her and her government cronies, but he couldn't let her be humiliated.

Stephen pointed to the scarlet T-shirt peeping out from underneath his sweatshirt.

'I forgot about this,' he winked, as Claudia heaved a sigh of relief. 'You owe me!'

A minute later, Stephen steadied the tranquillizer gun against his shoulder. The Pteranodon soon noticed the crude flag made up of a TV aerial and Stephen's T-shirt. The winged reptile swiftly soared in towards them as Stephen fired a shot – and missed.

'Try again,' Cutter instructed calmly, sweeping the banner above his head as Claudia stood nervously behind him. Stephen took aim, but once again the creature flew out of range.

'It keeps moving,' he mumbled, re-loading the weapon.

'Stephen, *shoot* it!' shouted Cutter, as the creature began dipping towards them once more. It was now just metres away.

'*Shoot it!*'

Claudia suddenly lost her nerve. She could see no way in which Stephen was going to stop this huge reptile that was heading straight for them. And she wasn't hanging around to be eaten.

As the giant winged reptile shrieked at the three humans standing on the rooftop, Claudia began to run, trying desperately to reach the exit at the other side of the building.

Behind her, a shot rang out as a tranquillizer dart connected perfectly with the belly of the Pteranodon soaring overhead. The creature crashed down, letting out an anguished cry as it skidded across the rooftop, heading directly towards Claudia as she tried to get out of the way. As she reached the roof's edge, Claudia turned round – watching in horror as the enormous body of the winged reptile slid swiftly towards her on its belly. She closed her eyes as its massive beak came to a halt just centimetres from her feet.

'What are we going to do with it?' she could hear Stephen asking Cutter. He sounded far too casual for her liking, so she cautiously opened her eyes.

'Take it back to the anomaly site,' Cutter was shrugging. 'Send it back.'

Claudia was fuming. What was *wrong* with these lunatics? Hadn't they noticed she'd almost been killed?

'That is *it*, Cutter. No more favours!' she interrupted furiously, still standing at the foot of the Pteranodon's beak. 'From now on, we do this my way. *I* make the decisions –'

But before she could say any more, a final muscle convulsion from the dazed reptile's body caused its great beak to spasm, flinging it up in the air and hitting Claudia square on the chin. She fell backwards and landed in a crumpled heap, knocked out cold.

Stephen and Cutter stared at her for a second, and realizing she was more stunned than hurt, looked at each other with bemusement. 'Whoops,' grinned Cutter, raising his eyebrows. At least this would keep her quiet for a while, but now what were they going to do with a stunned reptile *and* a stunned Home Office associate?

CHAPTER 7

Back at the golf club a short time later, Claudia finally stirred from her beak-induced stupor. As she lay on a stretcher in one of the main rooms, images of the Pteranodon flying towards her on the rooftop flashed through her mind. Claudia sat up in fright, her sudden movement knocking the blood drip lying beside her on to the ground. She swung herself round off the bed and threw her feet to the floor, not realizing the drip was directly underneath her until it was too late. The dark red contents burst out of the bag and seeped on to the wooden floorboards.

A slight breeze wafted through the afternoon air and Cutter was watching her from an open doorway.

'What happened?' she said, blinking.

'You took a knock. Nothing to worry about,' he said, guessing she was confused. He reassured her that she was safe, and back in the club house. Realizing she was awake, an SAS medic came in to check up on her. The doctor asked Claudia some standard questions to establish how she was feeling while Cutter picked up a small light from an array of medical equipment on the bench.

'I'll do some tests at the hospital,' the operative concluded, addressing Cutter. 'But I think it's nothing worse than a mild concussion.'

Noticing the leaking blood drip on the floor, the medic scooped it up and headed out of the room, leaving Cutter alone with Claudia. Cutter sidestepped the mess left on the floor and instructed Claudia to sit up straight.

Brushing back her long brown hair, he shone the torch into her dark eyes, trying to see if he could find any answers to her initial unsteadiness. Claudia's heart skipped a beat. She liked having Cutter there to take care of her.

'How are you feeling?' he asked, studying her beautiful face.

'OK,' Claudia replied quietly. Cutter's heart went out to her. She might be obstinate sometimes, but right now Claudia simply looked frightened. And he knew something was terribly wrong.

'Any nausea, any headache?' he continued gently.
'No.'

'Anything odd at all?' he persisted.

'Just the one thing,' Claudia whispered, her pretty brow furrowing. 'I can't *see* anything . . .'

Over in a clearing on the golf course, Captain Ryan was about to get a surprise of his own.

'I wouldn't get too close if I were you,' he was lecturing Stephen, as a flurry of SAS soldiers paced around the prone body of the winged reptile under a tarpaulin. 'That thing could come round at any time.'

Stephen looked at him wryly. Ryan might be a trained operative, but he obviously didn't know the first thing about knocking out a Pteranodon with a tranquillizer dart.

'She's going to be out for hours yet,' Stephen reassured Ryan. His face suddenly brightened as the very obvious sound of a bowel motion belched out from the other end of the Pteranodon.

'You have no idea how revealing dung can be,' Stephen said, as he ran towards the back of the tarp and reached underneath for the results. 'You can learn a lot from it.' He pulled out his hand, now holding a sloppy dinosaur poo.

Ryan's mouth dropped open in disgust as Stephen

Screeching loudly, the magnificent Pterandon swooped over the professor.

'Stephen, *shoot it*!' shouted Cutter, as the creature flew towards them once more.

Claudia, Cutter and Stephen brought in the dinosaur safely.

Connor and Abby found a mysterious patch of blood
in the lion enclosure.

As usual, Lester was being difficult.

Abby felt as though she was being watched.

Connor threw himself out of the car as the Future Predator smashed the windscreen.

Carrying the Future Predator's offspring in the crates,
the team walked through the Permian landscape.

'It's the camp we found the first time,' Cutter said
in amazement. '*We* made it.'

The past and future collided together in a mass
of claws and fangs.

Helen watched, horrified, as the SAS men
were picked off, one by one.

He would have to rewrite history, but Cutter vowed
to get Claudia back.

Lester often wished he had never met Nick Cutter.

dipped a finger into the muck and delicately licked it, looking thoughtful.

'That's just not right,' Ryan grimaced, looking green and shaking his head. He knew Stephen took his job seriously, but not *this* seriously.

The captain's top lip curled in revulsion as Stephen took another taste test. Something *else* just wasn't quite right. The lab technician would have to have a closer look underneath the tarpaulin for anything left in the muck, but Stephen was sure this dinosaur deposit contained the remains of a diet consisting of nothing bigger than lizards and fish.

Stephen's heart sank. If he was correct, then it could only mean one thing. Some other creature had come through the anomaly and attacked the golfer.

And the killer was still out there.

CHAPTER 8

Back in the woodland beside the green, Abby and Connor let out a cheer as Rex's mischievous chirp finally sounded through the trees.

Running around through the scrub, they saw the tiny Coelurosauravus perched on a log underneath a massive old oak tree. But Connor grew uneasy as he noticed something eerily familiar about the tiny dinosaur's behaviour. Rex's cheery chirps had rapidly become short, frightened barks as he flattened his body against the log, and the small reptile's head cocked to one side as he tried to see over Connor's shoulder. It was a look Connor had seen already from Rex today.

Abby and Connor slowly turned to follow Rex's line of vision as a chorus of unearthly squawks rang out above them.

There, lined up along almost every branch of the oak tree sat dozens of ugly, bird-like reptiles. They were Pterosaurs, but much smaller than the one that had swooped on Connor and Rex earlier on the green. Instead of a beak, they had short, carnivorous snouts filled with rows of needle-sharp teeth and piercing yellow eyes. Their leathery wings were a shimmering blue-black. Abby felt a shiver run down her spine. While the Pteranodon had appeared majestic, these things just looked downright evil.

Connor took a step back when one of the Pterosaurs on a lower branch let out a greedy cry as it picked up a scent in the slight breeze. Connor pulled Abby to the ground as the first Pterosaur launched itself from the branch towards them, followed by another and another, howling like a frenzied swarm of over-sized bats.

Within seconds it was over, Connor and Abby rising to their feet as the creatures flew off in the direction of the golf club.

Connor heaved a sigh of relief as a frightened Rex scurried in front of them, seeking shelter. Whatever prey those horrific beasts were after, at least it wasn't *them*.

Back in the club house, Cutter was trying his best to reassure a vulnerable Claudia. If only she would realize that she could trust him.

'Temporary blindness is a symptom of mild concussion,' he said, as Claudia stared straight ahead. 'You're going to be fine.'

Claudia nodded in agreement, but she didn't look convinced.

'Do you see anything at all?' Cutter asked.

Claudia looked around the room. She could just make out the blurry outline of wooden frames on the doorways and the bright sunshine streaming through dozens of glass panes.

Just then, Cutter's phone rang. It was Stephen.

'Listen, you know that hunch of yours?' the lab technician said, calling from the golf course. 'You were right. Old Leatherface didn't kill the golfer.'

Thank goodness they hadn't shot it, Cutter thought.

'The dung is the clincher,' Stephen continued. 'Just a few small reptile and some fish bones. That's it.'

'Exactly what I thought,' Cutter replied, his voice rising. 'It wasn't Connor it was after . . . it was *Rex*.'

Cutter's phone beeped, indicating it was about to run out of battery. Telling Stephen he'd ring him back, he finished the call.

'Did you catch any of that?' he said, turning back to Claudia.

'The Pteranodon is innocent,' she said contritely. Any closeness between herself and the professor suddenly seemed to be on the back-burner. 'What do you want me to do, pay compensation? You have to admit it – you made a lucky guess.'

'No,' said Cutter, quickly glancing out of the window and scanning the skyline. 'You're missing my point. If the Pteranodon didn't kill the golfer, then what *did*?'

At that very moment, a blood-curdling scream tore across the garden. Claudia's breath quickened as the reality hit her. The killer was still out there. And she could hardly see a thing.

'What was that?' she whispered frantically.

'I don't know,' Cutter replied, quickly moving to close the glass-paned doors as a precaution. 'Look, give me your phone.'

Claudia's brow furrowed. 'It's in my bag,' she said, desperately trying not to panic. 'In the car.'

'I have to get to a phone,' said Cutter. 'Just keep calm. All we have to do is keep all the windows and all the doors *shut*.'

'And we'll be fine,' he added, thankful Claudia wasn't able to see the alarm in his eyes. 'You're gonna be OK because *nothing* can get in here.'

Claudia nodded resolutely. Cutter could tell she was terrified, but if he didn't call for backup soon then they might never get out of here. He left the room, heading upstairs to try and find a phone.

Claudia took a few careful steps backwards, trying to find the edge of the stretcher. Her fingers gripped the sheet tightly, causing her knuckles to turn white.

'Everything's OK,' she muttered, trying desperately to calm down. Claudia's chest tightened as she thought she saw a small, black shadow flit past the glass doors that led out to the garden. Something was *definitely* out there.

Claudia clumsily felt her way over to the door, pulling on it to make sure it was shut. It was. She breathed a sigh as she leant her head against the glass panel in relief.

'*Raark!*'

Claudia screamed and reeled back in horror from the ear-splitting sound, as the tiny angry head of a small Pterosaur appeared at the window in front of her. Suddenly, hundreds of the creatures appeared and started launching themselves into the glass in a frenzied attempt to get inside the club house. Unable to see where she was going, Claudia tripped backwards, landing awkwardly in the sticky red blood that was still on the floor beside the stretcher. She could only see a hazy cloud of black, and hear the violent screeching. Then there was the terrifying sound of shattering glass as several Pterosaurs finally managed to crack the decorative windows. Looking up into the light, Claudia could dimly see their outlines flapping furiously, unable to manoeuvre their wings through the small panels.

Claudia trembled as she remembered the body she'd seen earlier. If Nick didn't show up soon, it looked as though she would end up like Andy the golfer.

CHAPTER 9

Suddenly, through the deafening screeches and chorus of splintering glass, she heard Cutter's calm voice. She felt his strong arms round her, pulling her up to her feet.

Cutter escorted her towards a doorway leading to the middle of the manor. Claudia screamed as a vicious Pterosaur finally made it through the window and hurtled towards them. Cutter threw her into the room ahead, pulling the door shut just as several of the flying reptiles crashed into the doorway after them.

'They just went crazy!' Claudia panted, speaking at a million miles an hour as they stood underneath the magnificent dome that topped the centre of the golf club. 'I slipped in the blood and then –'

'They can smell the blood,' Cutter interrupted.

'Like piranhas!' Claudia gasped, as the gravity of their situation finally struck her. 'Oh . . . have I got much on me?'

Cutter looked at her blood-soaked clothes, and then down at himself. In his hurry to pull her up from the floor, he'd also become covered in a significant amount of blood.

A violent tapping echoed above. Looking up, Claudia could see that the black mass from the garden had now swarmed above the glass dome skylight, frantically trying to find another way to get to their sweet-smelling prey.

As Cutter pushed Claudia out of the way, the winged reptiles finally punched their way through the glass and poured into the room. As he closed the doors behind them, Cutter knew the only way they could survive this was to get help. The line had been dead on the only phone he'd found upstairs, but perhaps he might be able to make it out to the car park. The professor racked his brains.

'I think there's one in the ambulance,' Cutter said urgently, sitting Claudia down on a small couch. 'I'll be back in a minute.' He looked at her anxious face and thought how pretty she was. What if they didn't make it out of here? He had to let her know how he really felt.

Without a moment's hesitation, he tenderly kissed her. And Claudia didn't seem to mind one bit.

'You're going to be safe here,' he promised and slipped out of the room.

Outside, the coast seemed clear. But as Cutter took a few more steps, a swarm of angry Pterosaurs suddenly burst out over the top of the manor. Cutter sprinted down a dirt path, through the woodlands leading to the road. Up ahead, he was horrified to see the body of the medic lying beside the ambulance. Without time to think, Cutter threw himself into the open back doors of the vehicle, pulling them closed behind him. The reptiles, maddened with blood-lust, hurled themselves against the windscreen, trying to get inside.

Cutter caught his breath as he spotted a phone sitting in the front cabin. Moving into the passenger seat, Cutter dialled Captain Ryan's number as a winged creature smashed into the window beside him.

'We're being attacked by a swarm of Pterosaurs!' he shouted, as the SAS operative answered the call. 'Claudia's trapped in the manor.'

Cutter shook his head as the ever level-headed Ryan instructed him to sit tight. What did the captain *think* this was? A fun day out in Blackpool?

'Hurry up!' Cutter yelled, as more flying creatures cracked against the sides of the ambulance. The glass wouldn't hold much longer.

Cutter moved to the back of the vehicle and began frantically rifling around the cupboards. Surely there was something he could use to keep the hungry Pterosaurs away from him. Cutter felt a wave of hope wash over him as he spied a gas bottle sitting on a ledge.

Checking he had his Zippo lighter in his pocket, Cutter inched carefully out of the back of the ambulance, expecting to be confronted by hundreds of winged creatures. But instead, only a couple came at him. He flicked the lighter at the gas bottle as a jet of flame shot out towards the creatures.

Cutter groaned as the burnt remains fell to the ground. If the full Pterosaur flock wasn't here, then they'd picked up another scent.

His heart sank. They had returned to the manor.

CHAPTER 10

Alone in the club house, Claudia sat quietly on the couch where Cutter had left her.

With her sight still blurry, Claudia's hearing was heightened, picking up even the tiniest sound. The quiet now was deafening, and Claudia hoped the silence didn't mean the creatures had followed Nick as he left the building.

She inhaled sharply as a spine-chilling squawk suddenly rang out nearby. Claudia stood up, ready to run. It sounded as though soot was falling down a chimney flue, which meant there must be an open fireplace in the room. Cutter hadn't noticed it and thought this room was safe. But it wasn't – there was an open avenue to the sky in here!

Claudia desperately felt her way along the wall. As she heard something coming down the flue, she felt a stack of golf clubs propped up against the wall next to the sideboard.

A foul Pterosaur flew into the room and clocked its prey. As it sounded a victory call to its family, Claudia knew the others would soon follow. As she pulled out a club, she was relieved to discover it was a long shot three-iron. She swung back and took aim.

'Hole in one!' she shouted triumphantly, as she successfully belted the grotesque shadow flying towards her. The Pterosaur hurtled across the room and crashed into the wall, dead. As Claudia looked back and tried to focus on the fireplace, a black swarm began shooting into the room, wailing like banshees.

As Claudia blindly swung at anything she could, a figure slipped unseen into the room and grabbed her from behind.

The frightened woman instinctively knew it wasn't Cutter.

'Who's that?' she shouted, trying to sound in control of the situation.

'Helen Cutter,' came the unexpected reply, as Claudia felt herself being dragged towards a doorway. She couldn't believe it. Of all people!

'What are you doing here?' she cried.

'You really want to discuss that right now?' came the infuriating reply.

From the erratic way she had been swinging the

golf clubs at the Pterosaurs, Helen could sense Claudia was having problems with her sight. The older woman led her into a corridor and slammed the door behind them. Claudia felt her way along the wall in front of her and started immediately down the hallway. The frenzied flock of Pterosaurs protested loudly behind them.

'Get in there!' Cutter's wife yelled, shoving Claudia through a door.

As Claudia stumbled into the new room, she could make out the outline of a stove and microwaves. She realized Helen had led them into the kitchens of the manor – just as the wave of small Pterosaurs swarmed down the hallway behind them.

'You're going to have to trust me,' Helen said, as she slammed the door shut and faced Claudia. 'It's either that, or a radical makeover from our friends back there.'

Claudia couldn't help but feel sceptical. Helen hadn't been particularly trustworthy so far, so why should she believe her now? After all, she had been missing for eight years until a few months ago, when she'd been discovered in one of the anomalies and forced to come back into the present. For almost a decade Nick had thought she was dead.

And then, even after intense questioning in the maximum-security wing of the Home Office, Helen had refused to answer any questions, instead disappearing into another anomaly at the first available opportunity. And here she was, magically reappearing again, asking Claudia to trust her.

Claudia sighed. Although her sight was slowly returning, her vision was still blurry. And she didn't know the first thing about these horrid reptiles, apart from the fact that they wanted to kill her. There really wasn't any other option but to let this woman help her.

Helen grabbed hold of her hand and led her past some large cooking ovens, before pointing to a door.

'Go and stand by it,' she commanded. 'When I say so, go out and close it behind you.'

'What are *you* going to be doing?' Claudia asked, watching as Helen ran back over to one of the ovens and started flicking on gas switches.

'Cooking!' came the reply, as Helen grabbed a tin jug and put it in the microwave. She pulled the kitchen door open.

Once again, the black swarm of shrieking, winged reptiles burst into the room, howling their fury.

'*Now!*' Helen suddenly shouted over the din.

Claudia turned the handle and let herself out, catching a final, blurred outline of Helen as she pressed the timer on the microwave and ran out of the other door.

Outside, seconds later, Cutter watched with horror as the manor windows in front of him exploded, shattering glass and sending the remains of hundreds of dead Pterosaurs flying across the garden. He'd been racing back to find Claudia, and now the manor was burning down right in front of him.

Sinking to his knees, he felt as though he had been punched in the stomach. He had lost her!

Footsteps crunched on the gravel behind him. Instinctively, Cutter could sense Claudia behind him.

Slowly, he stood up. 'You scared the life out of me,' the professor said, almost too frightened to look round. 'Are you all right?'

'I'm fine,' Claudia said quietly, as Cutter finally turned to face her. 'Helen saved me.'

Cutter's jaw dropped. 'Where is she?' he demanded, turning back to the burning club house.

'I don't know.'

'Is she still in there?' Cutter was now frantic. *What if Helen was dead?*

'She's gone,' Claudia replied in a daze, shaking her head. 'Like a ghost.'

Cutter sighed with disappointment. So Helen had disappeared again. There was so much he wanted to ask his estranged wife, it made his head spin. But past experience told him she would show up again. He just wished he knew when.

CHAPTER 11

Back in the woodland, Connor was still desperately trying to make amends with Abby over the Rex fiasco.

'Abby, I'm *really* sorry,' Connor said, genuinely upset. It didn't look like she was *ever* going to forgive him. 'I know I should have been more careful.'

Abby stared at him blankly. Was that it? That was the best he could come up with for nearly losing her precious pet?

Connor's heart sank. It was obvious she wasn't going to trust him ever again.

'I'll move out of the flat tomorrow,' he said finally, not able to look at her.

'Where are you going to go?' she asked, watching him as he kicked some dirt with the toe of his shoe.

'I'll be fine,' he shrugged. 'You know me.' Connor turned round and smiled at her shyly.

Abby looked at him for what seemed like an eternity. She sighed and rolled her eyes. They were friends, after all. Even though she was angry with him, she couldn't kick him out on the street.

'OK,' she said, taking a deep breath. 'Here's the deal. You do all the washing-up for a month *and* make me breakfast every weekend.'

Connor's face lit up like an over-excited puppy.

'Does that mean I can –' he stopped for a second. He was so happy he could hardly get the words out. 'Does that mean I can stay?'

'For now,' Abby corrected, closing her eyes. She hoped she wasn't going to regret this. 'Yes.'

'Oooh!' whooped Connor, grabbing Abby and lifting her up in a big bear hug. 'Thank you! *Thank* you!'

'I must be going insane,' Abby grinned. 'I quite like having you around!'

Connor's heart leapt. Maybe she was about to make his dreams come true and tell him how much she liked him?

'As a *friend*!' Abby added, reading his thoughts.

'As a friend,' Connor repeated, pretending he hadn't been thinking anything different. 'Buddies . . . what else?'

The two of them made their way back out to the course to find Stephen and Cutter. Behind them, half a dozen SAS soldiers, Claudia and Captain Ryan stood by as the giant Pteranodon began to wake. It was time to send her home.

Connor looked with a frown at the shimmer in the sky. The brightness it had radiated earlier in the day was beginning to fade.

'Guys,' he called. 'You'd better be quick. I don't think the anomaly's going to hold much longer.'

Claudia's mobile began to ring. Checking the number, she pressed the Cancel button and put the phone back in her bag. Cutter looked at her wryly until she admitted the call had been from her boss, Lester.

'What can I say?' she smiled, looking at Cutter innocently. 'The battery was down and I just didn't get to the call in time.'

'You're saying Lester doesn't know about this?' Cutter replied, secretly relieved that the government hadn't got too involved this time. Whenever Lester stuck his nose into dinosaur business it always made things more difficult.

'Wouldn't be happy if he did,' replied Claudia, shrugging her shoulders.

'I thought you weren't going to take sides?' he said, knowing he could now trust her.

'It's a one-off,' she grinned, knowing in her heart it wouldn't be the last time she helped him. The kiss in the club house had seen to that!

Stephen ran up beside them and handed Cutter the red flag he'd made earlier on the rooftop. It was time to entice the Pteranodon back through the anomaly, and this was one foolproof way to do it.

A giant crane had been parked in the middle of the fairway. It was the only way to get Cutter close enough to the anomaly and attract the Pteranodon's attention.

As Cutter jumped up into the small cage on the crane, Stephen turned and gave Captain Ryan the thumbs up. Ryan untied the rope around the carrier while Connor helped Stephen pull back the large green tarpaulin covering the enormous beast.

Now high up in the air, the professor was in position just beneath the anomaly. 'We're ready. Let her go!' shouted Cutter, holding the pole and letting the bright red flag unfurl in the wind.

As everyone watched, the dazed Pteranodon blinked and looked up groggily. Shaking her head, she slowly manoeuvred her massive body into a standing position, using her wings to prop herself up before stretching them out to their full capacity. As everyone watched in awe, the giant creature hopped twice across the trailer and then gracefully launched herself off the edge. As she began to glide off to the left of the golf course, the team called out to encourage the majestic Pterosaur to turn back in the direction of the red flag.

'Hey! This way!' Abby called, squinting into the setting sun as the silhouette of the prehistoric creature finally turned to the right and began looping in a final ascent towards the anomaly.

'Oh . . .' sighed Claudia, genuinely in awe of the flying reptile she'd been so scared of earlier in the day. She was so grateful her sight was fully restored and she was able to see this moment. Now she was finally beginning to understand what Cutter saw in these creatures. 'That's beautiful!'

Letting out one final farewell screech, the Pteranodon flew into the dazzling light in the sky behind her. The team on the ground watched in wonder as the tear in the atmosphere shimmered brighter for a moment and then snapped shut, leaving the sky clear, as if nothing out of the ordinary had been there at all.

On the ground, loud cheers rang out as they realized the Pteranodon had safely returned home. Abby and Stephen hugged as Connor tried unsuccessfully to indulge Captain Ryan in a high-five. It had been quite an incredible day.

CHAPTER 12

Several days later, Cutter stood in the middle of his office in the Department of Evolutionary Zoology at Central Metropolitan University. Spending so much time at the golf course had inspired him to concentrate more on his game and right now he was taking a putt, using a Sauropod bone as a golf club.

'Shot!' said a familiar female voice behind him appreciatively, as the ball successfully landed in a cup lying sideways on the floor.

Cutter turned round, smiling. He was usually happy to see Claudia standing in the doorway of his office, and today was no exception. She looked very pretty in her black business suit, her long brown hair sitting loosely on her shoulders. Cutter motioned for her to sit down.

'I've been thinking about Helen,' Claudia said immediately, wincing as she said Cutter's wife's name out loud. 'She saved my life. Things were much less complicated when she was just the enemy.'

Cutter smiled. He'd given up trying to predict Helen's behaviour a long time ago, and it made him uncomfortable to talk about it. Especially in front of Claudia.

Claudia watched him curiously, wondering how he *really* felt about his wife. But that wasn't the reason for her visit today.

'If we're going to defend ourselves,' Claudia began, 'we've got to discover *why* anomalies are opening and predict when the next one will appear.'

'Well,' Cutter mumbled, picking up another bone and testing its suitability. 'It may be possible to do that.'

'Are you going to tell me how?' Claudia asked, raising an eyebrow.

'I've got ideas, but I don't have any proof,' Cutter said, lining up a new golf shot. 'I need more time.'

He looked up as Claudia closed her eyes and frowned.

'Are you OK?' Cutter asked, suddenly concerned.

'Um, I haven't been sleeping well,' Claudia admitted, shrugging off his concern. 'Bad dreams.'

After the terror of the Pterosaur attacks, she'd been

having nightmares that saw her waking up in a cold sweat. But she didn't want to tell Cutter. After all, she was meant to be a cool and calm representative from the Home Office. She could handle it. And besides, she didn't want anyone thinking she was crazy.

In the Forest of Dean, the SAS had erected a large metal barrier around the site of the original anomaly where Rex and a Gorgonopsid had arrived from the past. Barbed wire was rolled out along the edge, with WARNING signs and red lights flashing at various intervals along the fence. No one was getting in or out of the site.

But as an SAS soldier patrolled the perimeter, a sudden sound – like metal tearing – made him look up towards the anomaly, which shimmered in the air. He quickly went over to it, cocking his gun as a precaution. But nothing seemed to have been disturbed.

The soldier spun round as the eerie sound seemed to swoop through the trees in the forest behind him. Going into a sprint, he bolted through the woodland and back to the perimeter fence where he'd been moments before. A massive hole had been torn through the barricade and the strong, metal bars jutted out like broken splinters. Someone – or some*thing* – had ripped through the steel like it was paper. The soldier immediately called on his walkie-talkie for backup, turning to scan the forest.

Behind him, a large black creature approached, creeping along the ground. With his back turned, the soldier never saw it coming – until it was too late.

'No trail, no footprints – nothing,' Stephen muttered, as SAS soldiers swarmed the Forest of Dean for the second time in several months. An hour had passed since they had found the damaged fence, and now the team was analysing the area.

'Are you sure you didn't miss anything?' asked Cutter, standing with Captain Ryan. As the dinosaur experts, he and Stephen had been called in when the radio operator lost contact with the soldier. Along with whatever had torn the gash in the fence, the soldier was missing as well.

'If there's anything out there we'd have found it by now,' Stephen said, trying to sound confident. He didn't relish the thought of a creature capable of slicing through metal running loose.

'Must've gone back,' Ryan shrugged, as if that was the end of the matter.

But Cutter had other ideas. He turned to look back at the gateway to a lost world, shimmering in the middle of the forest.

The creature that had ripped the hole in the fence had definitely come through the anomaly. And whatever it was, he was sure it hadn't found its way back home to the past just yet.

CHAPTER 13

'He made a mistake about Helen,' Claudia informed her boss as they walked down a hallway inside the Home Office. Claudia knew Lester's feelings towards Cutter, and she was busily trying to talk him round. But he seemed unconvinced.

'He should have told us about her.'

'He was under enormous pressure,' Claudia reminded him. 'If there's anyone that can help us predict and contain these things, it's him.'

Lester stopped and turned to face her. As usual, he was scowling as he cut straight to the point. 'How close is he to an answer?'

Claudia took a deep breath. 'I don't know,' she admitted.

Lester studied her for a second. He knew what she was trying to do, but it wasn't going to work. Cutter might be a so-called expert, but Lester still thought he caused more trouble than he was worth.

'Look,' Lester said dryly, his eyes narrowing as he gave Claudia a withering look. 'One day soon, an anomaly's going to open up and thousands of these creatures – maybe millions – are going to come pouring through. Let's hope he's made his mind up by *then*.'

Claudia's heart sank as she watched her boss turn on his heel and walk away. The outcome of their conversation was far worse than she had hoped.

Stephen walked through the grounds of the Central Metropolitan University. Cutter had asked him to go back and pick up some things to help with the investigation out at the Forest of Dean. As he walked along the pathway, he had the very real feeling that someone was following him. But when he turned, there was no one there apart from some students, on their way to classes. Stephen frowned. He must have been seeing things.

'In most eras of the world's history, you'd be dead by now,' said a voice close behind him.

'Helen!' Stephen said ruefully, turning round. 'What are you doing here?'

Cutter's wife stood before him, smirking. She was in the same khaki overalls and shirt she'd been wearing the last time he'd seen her, when she'd disappeared into the anomaly.

'All this urban living's made human beings such lazy animals,' she said, continuing with her tangent. 'Second-rate hearing, no sense of smell, no worthwhile instincts.'

Stephen eyed her warily. Every time they'd crossed paths since she'd turned up through the anomalies, she'd been so self-righteous – not at all like she was before her disappearance. Along with Cutter, she'd once been one of his teachers at the university, and together they'd been formidable scientists with unshakeable ethics. Stephen and Helen had known each other well back then, but now he could see that her attitude had changed. He could tell Helen had returned only because she had some sort of hidden agenda, and it annoyed him.

'Man has no predators,' he pointed out. 'We have nothing to be afraid of except each other.'

'Well, that *used* to be the case,' she agreed wryly. 'But times are changing, aren't they, Stephen?'

'Why don't you just tell me what you want?' Stephen asked bluntly as they walked inside to the university's cafeteria. He'd had enough of her already.

'A meeting,' she replied succinctly. 'With Nick and Lester.'

She handed Stephen a hand-drawn map and pointed at it.

'Tomorrow morning at eleven o'clock, here. No armed thugs, no ambushes,' she urged, looking him in the eye. 'They'll want to hear what I've got to say.'

'But they don't trust you.'

'I don't trust them either,' Helen retorted. 'But this is serious.'

Reaching into the rucksack she was carrying, Helen pulled out a newspaper and threw it on the table.

'Three people have disappeared in the last forty-eight hours,' she said, jabbing a finger at the front-page headline. 'I know what happened to them.'

Stephen scanned the newspaper article, quickly realizing it was connected to the crisis currently unfolding in the Forest of Dean.

'A creature,' he said out loud. 'What kind?'

Helen ignored his question. As far as she was concerned, the conversation was over. She stood up and hoisted her rucksack on to her shoulders.

With distaste, Stephen watched her leave. Whatever game she was playing, he'd have to wait until tomorrow to find out. The whole thing made him very uneasy.

Abby and Connor were crawling around the lion enclosure at Wellington Zoo. Abby had received a call at home saying one of the lions had gone missing, and they were looking for clues.

'At first we thought the lions had been fighting,' she said, as two other keepers and Abby's boss, Tim Parker, surveyed the scene. 'But none of them are wounded. Then we realized we'd lost one.'

They watched as the other two keepers and Tim stood arguing underneath a large hole, high up in the strong wire netting that covered the enclosure.

Connor pointed to a blood-spattered leaf on the ground.

'Looks like *something* got wounded,' he said.

Making sure they weren't being watched, he crouched down and took a blood sample with a swab he'd brought with him. Connor and Abby had seen enough strange creatures come through recent anomalies to know they should get evidence. If a dinosaur turned out to be responsible for the attack, then it might help them to identify it.

'There's no other proof, is there?' asked Connor,

placing the phial carefully in his pocket. 'All you've got is a missing lion.'

Connor snuck Abby a look out of the corner of his eye. She shook her head as she rested her chin in her hand, looking completely bewildered.

'Maybe he just ran away to join the circus?' Connor offered, trying to lighten the mood.

Abby gave him a shove, almost knocking him over. This was *serious*! When was Connor ever going to stop fooling around?

A short time later, Abby walked out to the elephant enclosure, carrying large buckets full of feed. Thunder rumbled in the distance as Abby nervously scanned the horizon. Something didn't feel right – it almost felt like she was being *watched*. Abby was relieved as the elephants came running for their food. If something *was* out there, at least it wouldn't attack her with such large animals around.

Meanwhile, Abby's boss picked up a call on his mobile phone as he juggled papers and his briefcase.

'Thanks for calling back,' Tim said, walking through some stables. 'No sign of the lion as yet. We're still hopeful, obviously.'

The park manager was too wrapped up in the call

to notice a large black shadow moving across the metal tops of the pens inside the shed. It moved swiftly, jumping over the gates and emitting a low-pitched, clicking growl. It didn't bear any resemblance to any of the creatures from the zoo.

Abby had been right when she felt something watching her. But the thing was no longer interested in the pretty zoologist. As it crept out of the stables, it was far more interested in Tim.

And it was hungry.

CHAPTER 14

Early next morning, Abby and Connor found themselves in a busy room of the Home Office, waiting for the other members of the team. Once again, Cutter had called them in to help with investigations.

'The blood analysis came back from the lab,' Connor said casually, reading the front page of the newspaper. 'Most of it was from a lion, but *some* of it was from a bat.'

Abby turned to look at him. She'd changed out of the zoo uniform and wellies she'd been wearing earlier, and was now in a simple T-shirt and jeans. Connor thought she looked amazing. Then again, Connor *always* thought Abby looked amazing.

'Bats get everywhere,' Abby replied, shrugging her shoulders.

'Yeah,' stressed Connor. 'But it was some really weird DNA. They said they'd never seen anything like it before.'

Abby pulled out her phone as a message beeped. It was from the zoo.

'My boss,' Abby said, frowning. 'No one's seen him since yesterday. They found his stuff, but there's no sign of him. He just *vanished*.'

The zoologist swallowed as she remembered feeding the elephants. She'd really felt like something had been watching her. And now here they were talking about a new anomaly, and Tim was missing. The whole thing was giving her the creeps.

She shook her head and decided it was time to go back to work. It was probably all a coincidence, anyway. Besides, if Tim wasn't around, they'd need all hands on deck to look after the animals today.

Elsewhere in the Home Office, Cutter, Stephen, Claudia and Lester stood talking about Stephen's encounter with Helen the day before. As usual, Lester was being difficult.

'Are you *sure* you don't already know what this is about?' he demanded, riling Cutter.

'Helen did save my life,' Claudia pointed out, trying to calm the situation. 'We should give her some credit for that.' Wringing her hands, she hoped to get Lester onside. Why did he have to be so difficult?

'And if she does know something about the disappearances . . .' she continued helpfully.

'That's a *police* matter,' Lester trumpeted, cutting her off mid-sentence. 'There's no evidence of creature involvement.'

'*Yet.*' Cutter said firmly. He was getting seriously frustrated. Here was Lester, a pasty-looking man who'd obviously never done a day of physical work in his life, wandering around in a freshly pressed suit and telling *him* how to run a dinosaur investigation!

'OK, fine,' Lester said reluctantly. 'But if this turns out to be another of her manipulative little schemes, the deal is off and she goes straight back on the wanted list.'

Agreeing to disagree, the group caught a lift down to the car park and began making their way to the outskirts of London. Following the directions on Helen's map, they eventually found themselves by a lake in woodlands not far from the Forest of Dean.

Right on time, Helen strode up the dirt path towards them. Lester watched her approach, scorn flashing in her eyes.

'You have a serious creature incursion,' Helen said, addressing Cutter first. 'A highly evolved ambush predator. Intelligent, adaptable and ruthless.'

'If there was a creature on the loose,' Claudia said haughtily, annoyed at Helen's abruptness, 'we *would* know about it.'

'At least three people have disappeared in the last few days,' Helen pointed out, staring at the woman whose life she had so recently saved. She was starting to regret it – Little Miss Home Office could be *very* irritating.

'Missing,' dismissed Lester, folding his arms resolutely.

'Killed,' corrected Helen. 'The creature has a lair somewhere nearby. It's taken them for food.'

'How do you know that?' asked Cutter sceptically. Helen had no right to come in and cause panic like this. Why didn't she just tell them what they needed to know?

'Because it nearly got me too.'

'*What is it?*' Stephen insisted, repeating his question from the previous day.

'It has no name,' said Helen mysteriously.

Cutter was beginning to get annoyed. Why couldn't she just be helpful for a change? Getting anything out of her was like getting blood out of a stone.

'Then which era is it from?' he asked, glaring at her.

'It doesn't come from *any* era,' Helen said, lowering her voice and stepping towards him until they were only centimetres apart. 'At least not one that can be identified yet.'

'I'm sorry,' replied Cutter, shaking his head. 'I don't understand.'

'Yes, you do, Nick,' Helen whispered, staring at him intently. 'You've known it ever since you first stepped into the past.'

Cutter's face fell as the realization hit him. If the creature wasn't from the prehistoric era, then . . .

'Are you saying we're being attacked by a creature from the *future*?' he asked, almost unable to get the words out.

CHAPTER 15

'I've seen a lot of amazing creatures, but nothing like this one,' Helen said finally. 'It has human levels of intelligence and an almost supernatural ability to stalk its prey. It could be right here now watching us and we'd never know.'

The group were all trying to deal with this startling news in their own way. Lester rolled back on his heels, deep in thought. Cutter and Stephen raised their eyebrows at each other. Claudia, meanwhile, was steadfastly refusing to believe Helen could be right. The woman was clearly mad as a hatter.

'If it's so clever,' she said with an air of superiority, 'how did you see it?'

'I discovered it in the Permian,' replied Helen, mentioning the prehistoric era that the Forest of Dean anomaly led to. 'Just after a kill. It was feeding and its defences were down.'

'What does it look like?' probed Cutter. If Helen

was finally talking, he was going to try and get all the information he could.

'Like a great ape. But bigger, faster and a lot more agile.'

'Hold on,' said Cutter sharply, realizing they were just relying on Helen's analysis so far. 'What makes you so certain that it's not some lost species that's just disappeared from the evolutionary records?'

Helen shook her head. 'It's not like any creature from the Permian – or any other – prehistoric era,' she said gravely. 'The only possible explanation is that it strayed through a future anomaly, into the Permian era and then on into ours.'

'How did it get here?' asked Claudia.

'I have no idea. It was only when I got back I found out it was on the loose. Obviously, my first thought was to do as much as I could to help.' Helen gave the group a winning smile.

Cutter eyed her suspiciously. She might have been missing for eight years, but he knew her well enough to be able to tell when she was lying. He knew Helen wasn't here because she wanted to be helpful.

'How public-spirited of you,' Lester sighed. 'Where can we contact you?'

Helen looked at Cutter, a calculating grin spreading

across her face. 'At my house, of course,' she said, challenging him.

Cutter baulked. Although she hadn't stepped through the front door of their place for eight years, it was true – it was still her house. Technically, they were still married and she had every right to be there.

Claudia looked on with a mixture of hurt and disdain. She'd thought a lot about Cutter kissing her in the golf club, and she really liked him. She couldn't help feeling that Helen knew it and was being a pain in the neck on purpose.

By mid-afternoon, Cutter and Helen were back at their house. Helen was casting a critical eye around the living room.

'You could've redecorated,' she said, as Cutter watched her from beside the piano.

'I like it,' he replied, smiling. He'd been expecting a comment like that from her. 'Are you going to tell me why you were lying?' he added.

'No idea what you're talking about,' Helen replied nonchalantly, pulling off her boots and leaning back on the couch.

'The others buy that line about you just wanting

87

to help,' Cutter began, moving over to sit in a red chair in front of her. 'But I've known you for longer than they have.'

Helen paused for a second. Her husband was right, and she realized the game was up.

'Look,' she sighed, picking up a familiar camera from the table. 'Everything I said about the Permian was true. I discovered the creature and made my observations. But I got too close – it sensed I was watching.'

Cutter watched her patiently. The pieces of the puzzle were finally beginning to fit.

'So you became the prey,' he figured.

'I only just got away,' Helen reminded him, hoping to elicit pity. 'The problem was, my escape route led me back here.'

'And it followed you,' Cutter groaned, finishing her sentence. 'So this is *your* fault.'

'I could've walked away,' Helen snapped, on the defensive now. 'But I didn't. I stayed to help.' She looked at Cutter, her face softening. 'I'm still human, Nick. I do care what happens. And I do care about you.'

Cutter wanted so much to believe her. But he couldn't help thinking that if she really cared about him, she wouldn't have disappeared without a trace for eight years.

She had so many questions to answer.

Sitting in the Department of Evolutionary Zoology office at the Central Metropolitan University, Connor was looking confused. Stephen had just told him about the meeting with Helen earlier in the day, and Connor couldn't understand why she'd been so scant on details about the new creature. He decided it was time to let Stephen in on his and Abby's discovery.

'I found some bat blood at the zoo yesterday,' Connor said hesitantly.

'So?' retorted Stephen as he rifled through some papers, only half paying attention.

'This bat blood had really screwed-up DNA,' he said, looking at Stephen anxiously. Stephen ignored him. 'I mean, it's probably nothing . . . but one of the lions went missing yesterday.'

Stephen looked up at him as Connor started spinning round in the chair, seemingly talking to himself.

'And now Abby's boss,' Connor continued, as Stephen put down the papers. 'He's just disappeared as well.'

'Where's Abby?' Stephen demanded, while Connor came to a stop. Connor was relieved to see Stephen was finally listening, but the serious look on his face made him nervous.

'She said she was working late,' Connor replied, as Stephen ran across the room to grab his jacket.

'Meet me at the zoo,' Stephen said, heading towards the exit and leaving a bewildered-looking Connor sitting in the office. 'With as much backup as possible!'

Connor frowned as Stephen bolted out of the door. What was his problem, all of a sudden? One minute he was talking about Helen and an alien creature from the future, the next he was running off after Abby.

Connor's jaw dropped as he realized what was going on. If the bat *wasn't* a bat, it was probably the future predator Helen had been talking about. And if the creature had been stalking prey at the zoo yesterday, it was probably still in the same area and looking for food.

And right now, Abby was there on her own.

CHAPTER 16

It was late afternoon, and Abby was watching the seals gliding through the water in their tanks. She was thinking about yesterday. *Something* had definitely been watching her and it freaked her out.

Abby drew a quick breath as the same feeling washed over her. She could feel something behind her. Gasping, she spun round – only to be confronted by a smiling Stephen.

She was so relieved she couldn't stop herself from punching him in the stomach. 'Don't creep up on me like that!' she cried.

'I wasn't creeping!' Stephen grinned. 'I was walking . . . normally!'

Abby laughed. She couldn't stay angry with Stephen for long – he was way too cute!

'Are you all right?' Stephen asked frantically as Abby frowned at him. 'There might be a creature here. We think it killed the lion and maybe your boss.'

Abby's head spun as she took in the news. She couldn't bear to think of Tim as a victim. But with the blood and DNA sample, it all made sense.

'The others are on their way,' Stephen added.

'You came here on your own just 'cause you were worried about me?' Abby asked, smiling.

'Well . . .' Stephen teased. He knew how Abby felt about him, and he had to admit he liked her company too. 'You and the sea lions – I'd hate it if anything happened to them.'

Abby felt like her heart was going to explode into thousands of pieces. As Stephen grabbed hold of her, she hoped for a second he was going to kiss her. But instead, he suddenly pulled her against the wall, indicating to her to keep quiet. A strange noise was coming from the end of the corridor.

As Stephen watched breathlessly, a large creature crept into view on all fours, its strange growl emitting a clicking noise as it sniffed the air through its enormous nostrils.

Abby's eyes were wide with fascinated horror. They'd seen a lot of strange things come through the anomalies, but *nothing* like this. Its black body was shaped like that of a great ape, only much leaner, with leathery skin and a wide, scaly ridge running down its back instead of fur. And rather than toes, it had a cloven claw at the end of each limb. Its eyes were small slits set wide apart on either side of its head, and as it bared its razor-sharp teeth, drool dripped from its mouth.

There was no doubt it was the Future Predator Helen had seen in the Permian.

Abby and Stephen didn't move a muscle. It moved closer, until they could smell the creature's rancid breath.

Then, without warning, lights flashed at the other end of the corridor as Captain Ryan and his men came running through the zoo. As Stephen pulled Abby to the ground, the beast leapt on to the wall just above them, swiftly making its way outside and back into the safety of the forest.

A short time later Claudia and Helen came face to face in the reception area of the zoo. The Home Office representative had been trying to give instructions to one of the SAS soldiers about sealing the area, but true to form, Helen was quick to interrupt.

'If you want to find its lair, you're going to need dogs,' she suggested breezily.

Claudia hadn't managed to talk to Helen one-to-one since the Pterosaur attack at the club house and decided now was as good a time as any. She asked the soldier to leave the room.

'You saved my life . . . thank you,' she said, addressing the scientist. 'Although now I come to think of it, you did leave it *rather* late.'

'You were doing so well without me,' Helen said sarcastically. 'It was only when Nick . . . ran off . . . that I thought I should intervene.'

'He didn't run off,' said Claudia, rising to the bait. 'He went to get help. He did everything he could to protect me.'

Helen glared at her younger rival. She knew Claudia and Cutter liked each other, and it irritated her. She might not have been a part of Cutter's life for a long time, but Helen didn't like thinking she'd been replaced.

'It's obvious you like him,' Helen continued.

'It's really none of your business!' Claudia replied hotly. Helen's attitude really bugged her. She couldn't just go abandoning her husband, work and friends for eight years, letting them think she was dead, and expect to pick up where she'd left off!

But this wasn't helping. Controlling her anger,

Claudia counted to three. 'Can we stick to the point?' she said, changing the topic. 'What can you tell us about this creature?'

'It's fast,' replied Helen. 'Incredibly fast. And it can camouflage itself in almost any environment. To survive in the Permian it's had to be highly adaptable, which is bad news for us.'

Helen shrugged her shoulders, keeping eye contact with Claudia as she continued speaking.

'Who knows? Maybe that's how humanity meets its end – by becoming the food source for a more successful species.'

Over in the woods beside the zoo, Cutter, Connor and Stephen were desperately trying to come up with a plan of attack. Unlike the situation with the Pteranodon, Cutter was sure that killing the Future Predator was the *only* answer. Captain Ryan and Helen walked beside them, along with dozens of SAS personnel and their dogs.

'This one's too dangerous,' he reasoned. 'If we kill it, we can't affect the past *or* the present.'

Without warning, a scream rang out across the forest. Soldiers rushed forward to the empty spot where one of their own had been standing just seconds before. An unearthly clicking noise drifted through the trees as several soldiers shot into thin air.

The sound was all around them now, moving through the forest at lightning speed. The Future Predator materialized on a branch directly above Cutter, allowing him to register its twisted features for the first time. But it didn't stay put for long. As the soldiers shot again, it vanished.

'We need a bigger gun,' Cutter gasped, catching his breath. His heart was racing. Somehow he knew the thing had been coming right for him.

As the group gathered together in a clearing, Cutter tried to keep his thoughts together. The creature seemed to be one step ahead of them all the time.

'I warned you it was smart,' Helen said, leaning casually against a tree and crunching into an apple.

'What we need is something that gives us an edge. Some weakness in its defences,' Stephen reasoned. 'Otherwise it's going to pick us off one by one.'

'The dogs went crazy before it attacked,' Connor remembered, as Helen smirked behind him. She obviously knew the answer. 'What'd make them go off like that?'

'It can't be smell,' decided Stephen. 'If there was a scent trail they'd have followed it.'

Cutter suddenly clapped his hands together. 'Hearing!' he shouted. 'That's why it managed to stay ahead of us. It can detect physical movement before it's within visual range!'

'And the dogs detect a higher frequency,' Connor said. 'They know when it's nearby.'

'High frequency soundwaves!' the professor nodded. 'It's like a sonar system. Some animals use it to detect prey.'

'Like a bat,' Stephen added carefully. 'So *that's* where the blood in the lion enclosure came in.'

'That's it!' Connor realized, getting excited. 'This thing must be some kind of . . . I don't know . . . *super-bat*!'

Helen had been watching the conversation with amusement. She seemed satisfied they'd finally figured it out.

But Cutter had a plan. Turning swiftly to Connor, he asked him to go and retrieve the oscilloscope from the truck. They'd be able to use the tracking device to find the Future Predator before it found them, then lure it into a trap and kill it.

Connor ran through the forest to the car park. He

97

found the oscilloscope thrown carelessly on the floor behind the driver's seat. As he switched it on, the machine began to beep incessantly.

Connor's eyes widened with panic. If the tracking device was registering a high reading, then it could only mean one thing.

The Future Predator was right there.

CHAPTER 17

Connor reached over and pulled the door shut. The truck shook as something dropped on to the roof. The student gulped as everything went quiet.

Connor reeled back in terror as the mutant head of the monster smashed through the front windscreen of the car, letting out a high-pitched howl of fury as it tried unsuccessfully to push its bulk between the seats to reach him.

He had to get out of there. Connor threw himself out of the side door, tumbling backwards into the dirt car park. But the creature quickly spotted him. In one rapid move it leapt from the bonnet of the car as shattered glass fell in all directions, hungrily pacing round the side of the vehicle towards him.

Suddenly, a voice rang out from the other side of the car park. Connor looked up with relief as Abby came running from the direction of the zoo. The Future Predator growled contemptuously at the interruption before turning back to Connor. Spit dripped grotesquely from its mouth. Without thinking, Abby picked up a rock from the ground and threw it, striking the creature's back leg.

Furious, the Future Predator turned and hurtled towards the missile thrower. Abby gulped. Desperate to save Connor, she'd forgotten she had nothing with which to defend herself. Now it looked like they were *both* going to become lunch.

Just as the creature crouched to dive at her, a single shot rang out. The Future Predator let out an ear-splitting cry, immediately retreating with several bounds back into the forest. Abby and Connor gasped for air as they watched Stephen lower his gun. That had been almost *too* close.

Connor turned to Abby as the two of them met beside the truck.

'You just saved my life!' he said, desperately trying to catch his breath.

'I had to,' she replied, trying to raise a smile. 'You haven't paid this month's rent yet!'

Connor sighed as Abby walked back to the zoo. Trust her to think of something like that at a time like this!

*

A little later, in a clearing in the forest, Cutter, Stephen and Helen watched the SAS swarm through a storage shed. Connor stood in the middle of them, holding the oscilloscope as it beeped wildly.

It wasn't long before they made a frightening discovery. There, in a makeshift nest on the floor, was a group of five tiny Future Predators, squealing in delight as they clawed and bit at each other. The creature had given birth – here in the present!

'*We've got company!*' Connor shouted, as the oscilloscope suddenly went into overdrive. A massive thud sounded on the roof above them.

Captain Ryan raised his gun towards a giant black shadow that was now darting around the room. But before he could shoot, the creature attacked one of the soldiers. Another soldier took aim and fired but it was too quick for him. Stopping for the briefest of moments, the Future Predator perched on a crate, ready to strike again.

Cutter's mind raced wildly. If he didn't do something now, this creature was going to kill them off one at a time, just like Stephen said. Without a second's hesitation, he grabbed one of the ugly, squealing babies from the nest and headed for the exit. The predator roared in outrage and took off after him.

Sprinting ahead, Cutter ran into a massive old greenhouse on the other side of the clearing. It had obviously been empty for a while, as weeds and long grass snaked along the sides. Cutter ran towards the far end of the building as the Future Predator appeared in the doorway. He desperately hoped his plan would work.

As the salivating creature began creeping forward, Cutter scanned the top of the structure around him. Then, with the Future Predator's baby shrieking in his grasp, he lifted his pistol and fired at a glass pane above the creature. As the Future Predator roared in anger, glass rained down upon it, confusing its sonar senses and ripping into its leathery hide. Cutter continued to shoot out the glass panels as the creature spun its head from side to side, trying to distinguish the shards of glass from its prey. Snarling, the Future Predator tried again to move forward. But the professor was too quick. Raising his pistol one final time, he took aim and fired.

With a heavy heart, Cutter prodded the lifeless body of the creature as its baby squirmed in his hand. Even though he knew the predator would have killed him given half a chance, he wished there had been an easier way to deal with it.

Now, the only thing left to do was to send the rest of these creatures back to the future.

CHAPTER 18

'If you kill them now, you'll be making a big mistake.'

Helen Cutter was with Lester and Claudia, striding down a corridor of the Home Office. Lester walked ahead with a scowl on his face.

'Then what do you suggest?' he quipped. 'A sympathetic foster family?'

'A dangerous anomaly to the future is open in the Permian,' Helen warned. She had no time for small talk with stiff government people like James Lester. 'Predators could come pouring through.'

'But why do we keep these animals alive?' asked Claudia, puzzled.

'To pinpoint the exact location of the anomaly,' Helen explained. 'All bats have extraordinary homing instincts. They'll know their own environment. They can lead us to it.'

'And what happens to them then?' asked Lester,

hating being caught up in all this dinosaur gobbledygook more by the minute.

Before Helen could answer, a familiar voice came from the doorway.

'We kill them,' Cutter said firmly as he walked into the room. 'To let even one of them loose in the Permian era could be a potential catastrophe. They could wipe out whole species – they could change things in ways we can't even conceive.'

'And afterwards we keep a permanent guard at the future anomaly?' Lester asked, for once genuinely interested.

'The threat's too serious to be ignored,' Cutter said earnestly, nodding.

'Serious enough to warrant a permanent intrusion into the past?' Claudia frowned.

Cutter looked at her curiously. Even though he knew she had to ask these questions as part of her job, he couldn't tell whether Claudia was on his side or not with this one.

'With the correct restrictions, yes,' he answered solemnly.

Lester sighed audibly. Not for the first time, he wished he'd never met Nick Cutter in the first place.

'All right, we'll do it,' he grimaced, turning away. 'I just hope you're right.'

Helen caught Cutter's eye as her mouth turned up into a smile. Claudia watched with envy as Cutter returned Helen's grin. She knew that no matter how interested she might be in the dinosaur phenomenon, she would only ever be an observer. Claudia could never hope to have the same scientific understanding Helen shared with Cutter, and their professional alliance made her squirm.

Late the next day, a team of SAS soldiers prepared to take the tiny Future Predators back into the anomaly. Helen and Cutter were hitching up their rucksacks, ready to make the trip as well. Cutter, as usual, was busy shouting instructions.

'Be careful with them,' he said, as two soldiers lifted the large steel box containing the shrieking baby Future Predators and walked into the shimmering light ahead of them. As always, the anomaly grew brighter for a second as the men went through.

Claudia walked up to the professor. She looked worried.

'What happens if it closes while you're on the other side?' she asked gravely.

'We wait until it reopens,' he said confidently, smiling at her. Claudia had the same vulnerable look now as when she'd lost her sight at the golf club. Cutter suddenly felt protective and wanted to reassure her.

As Connor, Abby, Stephen and several SAS soldiers studied equipment and tracking devices behind them, Helen jealously watched Cutter and Claudia from the other side of the clearing. Since her return, Cutter had made it very clear that he no longer considered her his wife, and it made her blood boil.

'I think we should get going,' she said loudly. She didn't want to give Claudia and Cutter any more time together.

Hearing Helen's instructions, Claudia suddenly grabbed Cutter's arm. Something about the bad dinosaur and anomaly dreams she'd been having made her uneasy.

'Don't go,' she said urgently. Cutter looked surprised. 'I think this is a mistake. I've got a really bad feeling about this.'

Cutter looked at her calmly. 'It'll be fine,' he said quietly, his green eyes sparkling warmly. 'I'll see you soon.'

Cutter picked up his bag and made his way to the anomaly. Claudia watched him go. Even after their conversation she didn't feel any better. Something wasn't right.

Elsewhere in the clearing, it was Abby's turn to feel uneasy. She'd just noticed Helen catch Stephen's eye as she waited by the doorway into the Permian era. Something about the familiar way they looked at each other made her anxious. It was only a fleeting glance, but it was almost as if they had an understanding. Abby frowned. Maybe she'd just been imagining things.

As Cutter and Helen turned to follow the SAS through the anomaly, Claudia couldn't hold herself back. If Cutter wouldn't stay, she at least needed to let him know she hadn't forgotten what happened at the golf club. Claudia ran and kissed the surprised professor. Cutter smiled at her and then kissed her back, as Helen scowled at them with contempt. Everyone else just looked on in astonishment. No one knew about their kiss in the club house, and they certainly hadn't been expecting this!

As the group disappeared through the shards of light, Connor's mobile rang. After a hurried conversation, he hung up the phone looking confused.

'The creature's autopsy proves beyond any doubt that it was definitely a male,' Connor said, frowning.

Stephen shook his head, trying to make sense of it. The creature *had* to be female – it had given birth! And if it wasn't, then that meant the creature Cutter had killed in the greenhouse wasn't the only Future Predator to get through the anomaly.

Over on the table, the oscilloscope suddenly began beeping again, going into overdrive as a dark shadow paced through the scrub. Stephen thought he saw a blur shoot past out of the corner of his eye, but as he spun round, nothing was there. Abby shivered. Once again, she could feel a presence watching her. A second later, all three of them turned in the direction of the anomaly, as it let out a bright glimmer, just as it did every time something went through it. But surely they would have realized if something *had* gone through?

Stephen breathed in sharply, knowing from his encounters with the first Future Predator that it moved fast. There was a chance another could have just darted through the anomaly without any of them seeing it. And if there really was a female creature on the loose, she'd be looking for her babies.

'Did you see something?' Claudia asked urgently, striding across the clearing as the SAS soldiers raised their weapons. She felt like she was about to snap.

This whole thing was just getting weirder by the second.

'Nothing,' replied Stephen honestly, as Connor held his compass up and confirmed the anomaly was stronger than ever. He just hoped something else had unsettled it.

CHAPTER 19

Inside the anomaly Cutter was looking around in utter fascination. He'd been here before, but the Permian era still took his breath away – it was incredible! Finding himself in a landscape created over 250 million years ago, the professor scrunched up his nose as the familiar smell of rotten eggs wafted faintly through the air. Everything was exactly as he remembered it.

Gazing in wonder at their dry, barren surroundings, Cutter helped Helen, Ryan and the SAS soldiers make camp among a sparse green patch of vegetation and shrub. It was a change from the vast stony hillsides they'd trekked over to get here, and allowed them at least some protection from any creatures that might come across them. The soldiers had dumped their heavy supply boxes, leaving the crate of baby Future Predators sitting beside some equipment in the sun.

Helen rolled down the top of her overalls and stood

in a dark khaki singlet and neck scarf, taking photos with the camera she had found on the table at Cutter's house. She'd recognized it as her own, and realized Cutter must have picked it up when he travelled through the anomaly and into the Permian era the first time. It was good to have it back again.

'Hey, Nick!' she called out from her vantage point on top of a hillside. 'Come here!'

Cutter excused himself from his conversation with Captain Ryan and walked through the maze of rocks embedded in the ground.

She threw her camera to him and smiled. 'May as well take a souvenir,' she grinned, posing.

Cutter held up the camera and looked through the viewfinder, trying to include the distant herd of giant Gorgonopsids in the shot. Cutter thought back to several months ago when he'd seen one walking through the Forest of Dean. It was the first dinosaur to come through any of the anomalies. The professor smiled. They might look cumbersome and harmless right now, but they were carnivores and could attack and move with deadly speed.

Taking the photo, Cutter suddenly froze. He'd seen that exact picture before. Helen frowned at the fearful look on his face.

'What?' she asked, curious.

Cutter's mind raced. The photo, the camera, the camp . . . *everything*. He'd seen it all the first time he and Captain Ryan came through the original anomaly in the Forest of Dean, when they'd tried to return Rex and had begun searching for Helen in the first place.

Cutter's eyes grew wide as he remembered something else. There had been a skeleton buried there. If they'd all been here before, then the bones belonged to one of them!

'The camp,' he stuttered, looking at Helen wildly. 'It's the camp we found the first time. *We* made it.'

Cutter raced down the hill towards the supply box, as Helen watched quizzically. She didn't understand what he was talking about.

'It's us!' he shouted as he came level with Captain Ryan. '*We're* the intruders.'

'The camp we found was old,' Ryan reasoned, thinking back to the tattered tents and rusty supply boxes they'd seen. 'There was a dead body,' he added, wondering whether Cutter had finally lost it.

'Don't you see?' Cutter said, rifling through a supply box and pulling out objects they both recognized from the first trip. 'We've arrived back years *before* the first time we came here.'

113

Ryan looked at him in shock as Helen came down from the hillside. Cutter stared at the soldier in horror. 'We've created our own past!'

Before Ryan could reply, a storm of protest erupted from the crate holding the ugly babies. Ryan motioned to his men as all the SAS soldiers raised their weapons. Something was out there.

'We must be near the anomaly!' Helen cried, believing the tiny predators were shrieking for another reason. She picked up her rucksack, ready to begin the search. 'This is it, Nick,' she whispered, a look of greed suddenly spreading across her face. 'We've found it. We've found the future!'

Cutter recoiled in horror as the truth finally dawned on him. She'd had a hidden agenda all along. Helen hadn't returned to the forest to help them find the predators at all – she'd come back because she knew they could lead her to a world beyond the present.

'That's all you cared about,' Cutter said incredulously. 'You just wanted to find the future for yourself!'

Helen smiled at him shrewdly. Hitching up her rucksack, Helen walked over to join the soldiers, looking over her shoulder at Cutter with a smirk.

Helen was just a metre away when the female

Future Predator struck, tearing into a soldier just ahead of her. Just as Stephen had feared, the dead predator had not been alone. Following the cavalry carrying the crate of squawking babies through the anomaly, the mother predator had finally caught up with them. And now she wanted revenge.

As the creature's babies shrieked furiously, the remaining soldiers scrambled for position. For once, Helen was completely taken off-guard.

The evil predator swiftly began to pick off the men one by one before moving back to the crate, splitting open the box to release her young. Captain Ryan sprinted forward, successfully shooting the creature as the ugly babies crawled around it.

But the Future Predator wasn't going to be taken down that easily. Full of fury and adrenalin, it leapt forward and knocked Ryan down, dragging him along the stony hillside in its jaws. Cutter watched in horror. He and Ryan had been through so much together – was this the end for all of them?

Sensing someone watching it, the creature looked up, locking eyes with the professor. Losing interest in the prone soldier, it bounded across the landscape, snarling viciously at Cutter as it crept towards him. He braced himself for the strike.

But it never came. Suddenly, the creature let out a howl, looking into the distance behind his victim. Cutter turned in confusion, as a mighty roar sounded. A massive Gorgonopsid loped into the clearing, attracted by the scent of fresh blood it had picked up. As Cutter caught his breath, the dinosaur charged towards the predator, past and future colliding together in a mass of claws and fangs.

The power of the hungry Gorgonopsid easily outweighed that of the injured Future Predator. Rearing its head, the prehistoric carnivore caught the creature in its powerful jaws, throwing it like a rag doll into the air.

The female predator lay groaning on the ground as the Gorgonopsid spied the baby predators wriggling out of the crate. Sensing an easy kill, it began devouring the squealing creatures, one by one.

Without warning, the furious Future Predator recovered, desperate to protect its offspring. Its savage teeth ripped into the Gorgonopsid as it sprang on to the back of the dinosaur, both creatures fighting for supremacy. Baying for blood, the howling Future Predator clawed repeatedly at the tough hide of the hapless Gorgonopsid, leaving huge gashes in the larger creature.

116

As Cutter crawled silently towards Captain Ryan, it looked like the predator was going to prevail. But in a blur of twisted limbs and confusion, the monolithic Gorgonopsid reared up angrily as the Future Predator clung on, landing on the creature as it fell backwards and crushing it to death.

Sounding a victory cry, the embattled Gorgonopsid grasped the remains of the Future Predator in its jaws. Ignoring the last two humans, it made its way through the destroyed campsite and into the forest to devour its prey.

Turning back to the injured Ryan, Cutter desperately tried to comfort him. The captain looked up at him as he lay on the ground, his face racked with fear and understanding. Ryan tried to speak as he gasped for air. 'The first time we came here, that body we found . . . that was me, wasn't it?'

Cutter said nothing. They both knew the dreadful answer.

'I was looking at myself . . .' finished Ryan sadly, as he closed his eyes and took his last breath.

With a heavy heart, Cutter looked over to Helen. She was inspecting the tiny bodies lying on the ground around the crate.

'It looks like they're all dead,' she decided, not

seeming to care about the carnage they'd just witnessed.

'This is over,' Cutter said firmly, as Helen came over to him. 'We should bury the men and then we're leaving.'

But Helen had no such plans.

'We don't have to go back, Nick,' she whispered seductively. 'The future anomaly must be here somewhere. We can still find it!'

Cutter shook his head. Her greed and stupidity had already caused the death of so many people. What was she thinking?

'If you want to stay here and look for it, that's fine,' he said, picking up his rifle and looking towards the horizon. 'But you're going to have to do it on your own, because I'm leaving.'

Helen's mood suddenly darkened. It was obvious to her that Nick was going back because of Claudia. The very thought infuriated her.

'I know where I belong,' Cutter added, standing up. He just wanted to get through the anomaly and go home.

Helen looked at him for a second, trying to figure out her next move. She was still determined to find the anomaly into the future. But perhaps there was one final thing she could wrap up in the present first.

She picked up her rucksack and followed Cutter as he headed back across the stony barren landscape of the Permian era. Cutter focused straight ahead, barely looking around him. The ancient landscape no longer fascinated him.

Behind them, way up on a hillside, two squealing creatures watched the scientists leave, darting through rocks and clawing at each other.

For once, Helen had been wrong. Some of the baby Future Predators were still alive.

CHAPTER 20

Abby and Connor sighed with relief as Cutter came walking through the anomaly back into the Forest of Dean. But there was something about his expression that made them worried.

'What happened?' asked Lester, his arms folded impatiently. 'Did you find the anomaly?'

Cutter shook his head gravely as Helen appeared behind him. They were alone.

'Captain Ryan didn't make it,' he said solemnly. 'All the men are dead.'

The SAS soldiers looked visibly distressed.

'Whatever happens,' Cutter said, wanting to finish it once and for all, 'nobody goes back through.'

'Well!' huffed Helen behind him, walking away from the anomaly and into the clearing. 'I'm sorry to break your new rule so soon Nick, but I'm not staying.'

Cutter stared at her in confusion as she strode

purposefully over to Stephen. What was she up to now?

'You see, I don't want to be alone any more. And you once said you'd do anything for me if I gave you the chance,' she said, smiling at the younger lab technician. Stephen glared at her angrily. 'Here it is. Come with me.'

It was obvious from the way she approached him now that there was unfinished business between them. Before her disappearance eight years ago, it seemed that she and Stephen had been more than just good friends. Both Abby and Cutter were shocked.

'Well?' demanded Helen, smirking at Stephen. 'Are you coming?'

Stephen turned to look at Cutter. The professor returned his gaze, completely dumbfounded. He hadn't known about a relationship between Helen and Stephen. Even though he didn't love Helen any more, Cutter felt like he had been slapped in the face. Why was she trying to make Stephen, his closest ally, swap sides?

But the younger man was having none of it. Any romance with Helen was in the past. Without saying a word, he glared at her before rejoining the group, making his loyalties clear.

Helen frowned. Turning to study the other individuals standing around the anomaly, she hoped to find a friendly face. But instead, everyone in the clearing looked back at her with sadness in their eyes. Every time she'd come through an anomaly she'd caused nothing but pain. Now they just wanted her to go for good.

Helen's face was a mix of coldness and confusion. Giving Cutter one final look of defiance, she turned on her heel and stormed back into the anomaly.

Cutter looked at the ground for a second. He didn't know quite what to make of the last few minutes and his head ached. But something else irked him.

Someone was missing.

'Where's Claudia?' he said suddenly, his eyes darting around the clearing. 'Where's Claudia Brown?'

Lester looked at him, puzzled. Maybe he'd bumped his head in the Permian.

'I don't know anyone of that name,' he said, surprised to see Cutter stick out his jaw.

'No, come on!' shouted the professor, suddenly agitated. This wasn't funny.

'We don't know what you're talking about,' Stephen said calmly, shaking his head.

'Never heard of her,' added Connor.

Cutter was stunned. A nauseating wave of panic began washing over him, quickly replaced by a bubbling rage.

'Look,' he said, trying to stay calm. 'You've been working with her every day for months, so don't tell me you don't know who she is!'

'No idea,' Lester shrugged, wondering what on earth had got into the man. 'Sorry.'

Cutter snapped. If this was Lester's idea of a joke, it was pathetic. He strode over to the stunned government representative on the other side of the clearing and grabbed him by the lapels of his business suit.

'*Where is she?*' he shouted, as the remaining SAS soldiers raised their weapons.

'Cutter!' Connor urged. 'We don't know her!'

Cutter glared at Lester for a second before letting him go. He closed his eyes. It was all too much.

'This isn't right,' he muttered. 'Something's happened.' Cutter turned to look at the bewildered group standing in front of him. He felt sick.

'Something's changed!' he sounded distraught. 'We've done something!'

Cutter's voice trailed off as he grappled to make sense of it all.

'Something that we've done has changed the past and she's not here any more!' He willed the others to believe him.

Cutter's heart sank as he realized that once again, he would have to go back through the anomaly and change the course of history. As he looked around the alarmed faces in the clearing, Cutter knew the problem was going to be convincing the others he was telling the truth. How could he explain what Claudia meant to him? To all of them? They'd never even met her.

Behind them, the blinding shard of light seemed to grow stronger, pushing bright beams out across the forest. Cutter sighed as he turned to watch it. For something so dangerous, it really did look beautiful.